Where Is Papa Now?

Celeste Conway

Boyds Mills Press

Published by Caroline House
Boyds Mills Press, Inc.
A Highlights Company
815 Church Street
Honesdale, Pennsylvania 18431
Printed in Mexico

Publisher Cataloging-in-Publication Data
Conway, Celeste.
Where is Papa now? / [by] Celeste Conway.—1st ed.
[32]p. : col. ill. : cm.
Summary: A mother and daughter imagine all the places Papa is visiting
on the clipper ship *The Lucky Goose*.
ISBN 1-56397-130-5
1. Family life—Juvenile fiction. [1. Family life—Fiction.] I. Title.
[E]   1994
Library of Congress Catalog Card Number 92-74584   CIP

First edition, 1994
Book designed by Celeste Conway
The text of this book is set in 16-point Zapf Calligraphy.
The illustrations are done in cut paper.
Distributed by St. Martin's Press

10 9 8 7 6 5 4 3 2

To Peg Conway,
my mother

It was springtime when Eliza's Papa went to sea.
He was captain of a tall white ship called *The Lucky Goose*.
Mama was sad to see him go. She stood at the door
and waved good-bye. Eliza blew kisses down the hill.

Time went by.

"Where is Papa now?" Eliza asked her mother
as they watched from the window one starry night.

Mama closed her eyes.
"He is in hot Java buying puppets
and coffee and sugar cane.
He is riding in an ox-drawn cart
over a skinny bridge."
"When will he be home?"
"Soon, child, soon."
"Hurry, ox," Eliza prayed.
"Hurry and be safe."

Summer passed. The leaves on the trees
turned red and gold.

"Where is Papa now?" Eliza asked her mother
as they listened to the wind.

Mama drew Eliza close.

"He is in China buying tea and rice and ginger jars.
He is riding on a Chinese horse."

"When will he be home?"

"Soon, child, soon," said Mama.

"Hurry, horse," Eliza prayed.

"Hurry and be safe."

Winter came. The trees were bare and the sky was dark. "Where is Papa now?" Eliza asked her mother as they worked in the kitchen beside the fire.

Mama looked out at the swirling snow. "He is in Bombay buying pepper and jewels and golden cloth. He is riding on an elephant by a river filled with stars."

"When will he be home?"

"Soon, child, soon."

"Hurry, elephant," Eliza prayed.

"Hurry and be safe."

Spring came again. Shoots pushed up through the
hard brown dirt, and the trees were green with
buds. Eliza turned six years old.

Spring became summer. The flowers bloomed
and the skies were blue.
"Where is Papa now?" Eliza asked her mother
as they sat in the sunny garden.

Mama gazed past the roses. "He is sailing on an
angry sea. The wind is wild and the waves are fierce.
The Lucky Goose is trembling."
"Oh, when will he be home?"
"Soon, child, soon," said Mama.
"*Lucky Goose*, steady," Eliza prayed. "Steady and be safe."

The leaves turned red and gold once more, and Eliza started school.

"Where is Papa now?" she asked as she practiced writing her name one night.

The jack-o'-lantern flickered as Mama pointed to the sky. "Do you see the North Star? He is sailing in its calm, white light."

"When will he be home?"

"Soon, child, soon."

"Burn, star, burn," Eliza prayed. "Burn and bring my Papa home."

The weeks went by.

"Where is Papa now?" Eliza asked her mother as they snuggled under the winter quilts.

"Look out the window," Mama said. "Look far as you can, and you will see the snow-white sails of *The Lucky Goose*."

"But when will he be home?"

"Very soon, my child."

"Hurry, white sails," Eliza prayed. "Hurry and bring my Papa home."

The days went by.

"Where is Papa now?" Eliza asked her mother as they carried home the Christmas tree.

Mama looked down the snowy cliff. "*The Lucky Goose* has anchored in the harbor. The sails are down and all is safe. The men are rowing toward the shore."

"But when will he be here?"

"Very, very soon, my child."

"Hurry, rowboat," Eliza prayed. "Hurry and be safe."

The hours went by.

"Where is Papa now?" Eliza asked her mother
as they warmed the tea and laid the food.

"He is very close. Get your cloak so we can go and
meet him on the hill."

"When will I see him?"

"In just a little moment, child."

"Hurry, moment," Eliza prayed.

WELCOME HOME PAPA

The seconds ticked.

"Where is he, Mama?" Eliza asked as they scurried down the icy path.

"I am here," said Papa, coming over the hill. "I am home at last, beloved child."

"Hurry, feet," Eliza prayed, running to her Papa's arms.